First published in Belgium and Holland by Clavis Uitgeverij, Hasselt – Amsterdam, 2008
Copyright © 2008, Clavis Uitgeverij

English translation from the Dutch by Clavis Publishing Inc. New York
Copyright © 2012 for the English language edition: Clavis Publishing Inc. New York

Visit us on the web at www.clavisbooks.com

I Have Two Homes written by Marian De Smet and illustrated by Nynke Talsma
Original title: *Ik woon in twee huizen*
Translated from the Dutch by Clavis Publishing
English language edition edited by Emma D. Dryden, drydenbks llc

ISBN 978-1-60537-102-3
This book was printed in September 2011 at Proost, Everdongenlaan 23,
B-2300 Turnhout, Belgium

First Edition
10 9 8 7 6 5 4 3 2 1

Marian De Smet | Nynke Talsma

I Have
Two
Homes

Clavis

NEW YORK

I am Nina.
I live in two homes.
Dad lives in one house.
Mom lives in another house.
And I live in both houses,
sometimes with Mom and sometimes
with Dad.

It used to be different.
I used to just have one home
with Mom and Dad both in it.
Cat had her basket under the stairs
and my hamster's cage was by the window.

Mom and Dad were happy together then.

They gave each other hugs and kisses when they got home every day.

I would stand between them like a hotdog in a bun.

But then things changed.

Dad did things Mom didn't like.

And Mom shouted words that made Dad sad.

Then there were fights and they would stand very far apart. Too far apart for me to fit, so I'd crawl into a tent under the table.

One day, our home became too
small for the two of them.
So there had to be two houses:
One for Mom.
One for Dad.
And two for me.

Everything is different now.
Everyone is acting strangely.
At Mom's house, Mom talks to Grandma
for a really long time and Grandma forgets I'm
even there. I knock over my glass, kick the chair,
and mess around with lipstick. Mom doesn't get
angry and Grandma pats me on the head.

At Dad's house, Dad is sitting on the couch.
I throw a blanket over his head. Now he is a ghost.
"Help!" I yell and I start to run away.
"Boo!" Dad says. "Boo!"
But it doesn't sound scary. It sounds sad.
He is a sad ghost.

When I am with Dad, I want to be with Mom.
I miss my hamster and the climbing tree.

When I am with Mom, I want to be with Dad.
I miss Cat and my friend from next door.

I speak to Mom and Dad every day.

At Mom's house, I call Dad and he asks how things were at school.

At Dad's house, I call Mom and she wants to know what I had for dinner.

I give them kisses through the telephone and I always get kisses back.

The kisses tickle my ear.

I get to celebrate my birthday twice. I have two parties, one at Mom's house and one at Dad's house.

But when I jump into the deep pool at school for the first time, Dad and Mom are both there.

Mom and Dad aren't happy with each
other anymore. But I know they are very happy
with me.

"That will never change, my sweet girl,"
Mom says, and she gives me a big kiss.

"That is forever, my precious one,"
Dad whispers, and he hugs me tightly.

I am Nina.
I have two homes.
It's strange.
But it is nice, too.